Keeping it

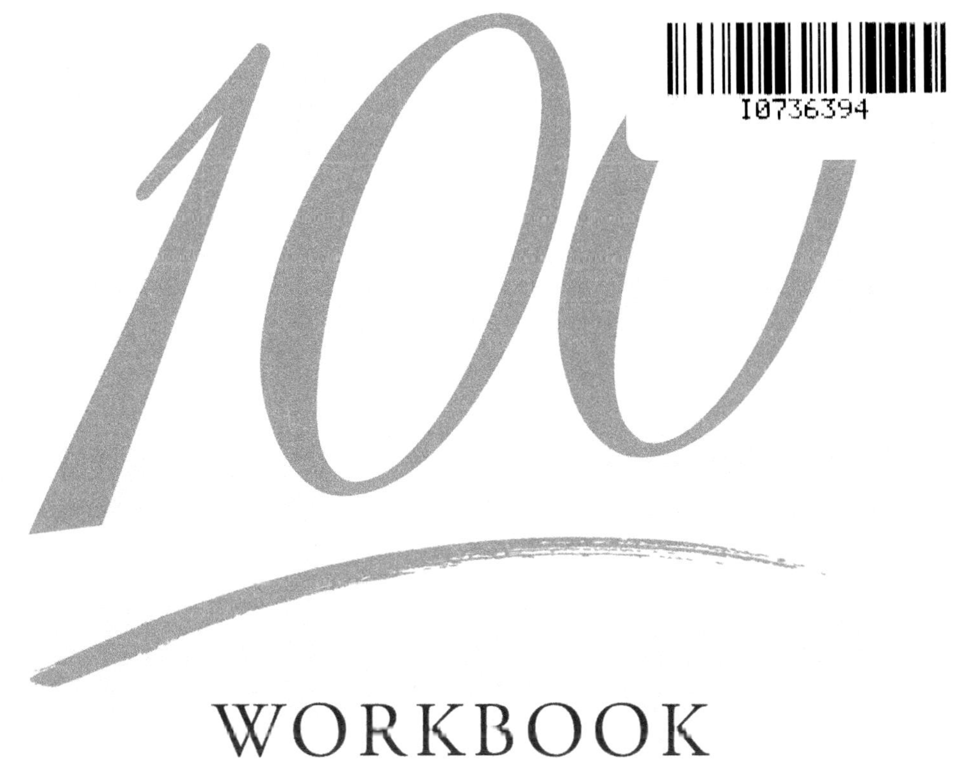

WORKBOOK

A YOUNG WOMAN'S GUIDE TO PERSONAL GROWTH

NINA MICHELLE

Keeping it 100 Workbook
A Young Woman's Guide to Personal Growth

Self-Published by:
NyreePress Literary Group
www.nyreepress.com

ISBN paperback: 978-1-945304-99-6

Inspiration / Woman's Inspiration

Printed in the United States of America

INTRODUCTION

It has been a year since God used me to publish the book Keeping It 100: A Young Women's Guide to Personal Growth, and I am overjoyed! But after all the reviews and readings that have taken place God placed it on my heart that there needed to be more. God said that people need to have a dialogue with themselves through this book. They need to write their truth! People need the opportunity to be honest and get to the root of the things that are plaguing them. This workbook is for YOUR EYES ONLY!!! Be honest with yourself! God gave me this workbook to breathe life into you and your situations.

This is the start of your NEW BEGINNING! Be Blessed!!

Keeping It 100:
You are <u>not</u> a statistic

1. Do you come from a single parent home? Do you have a relationship with the parent that you did not live with? Do you have positive relationships with your parents? Do you feel safe and secure with your parents? Write your truth.

    ____
    ____
    ____
    ____
    ____

2. Can you relate to a feeling of lack? How has that shaped your perception of life? Do you feel like you have "enough?" Write your truth.

    ____
    ____
    ____
    ____
    ____

3. Do you have a moment from childhood that is vivid in your mind? What does that moment entail? Was it a happy moment or a sad moment? How has that shaped who you are? Write your truth.

____

____

____

____

____

4. Do you feel like you are following in the footsteps of your family? Is this a good direction to go? Is this what you want for your life? Can you see yourself doing something else? Write your truth.

____

____

____

____

____

5. Do you feel like you are carrying some emotional baggage from your past? Do you often wish things in your life were different? Do you try to find happiness outside of yourself? Why do you do this? Write your truth?

____

____

____

____

____

6. Do you feel like you are always in the same place, doing the same things, with the same people? Do you feel like there is more to life than what you are currently experiencing? Write your truth.

____

____

____

____

____

7. Did you know that you are speak things into existence in your life? Did you know that life and death lies in the power of your tongue? Speak three nice things about yourself and where you are going in life? (Ex. I am beautiful. I am an overcomer. I am going to walk in God's purpose for my life.) Write your truth.

____

____

____

____

____

8. What can you do right now to change your present situation regarding this topic? Write your truth.

____

____

____

____

My thoughts / revelations about what I wrote in this section…

Additional Thoughts / Reflections

Additional Thoughts / Reflections

Keeping It 100:
Expectation vs. Reality

1. What is your definition of a Bad B****? Do you feel like this expectation is too much to ask for? Do you find yourself trying to live up to societies norm and forgetting what God said about you? Write your truth.

____

____

____

____

____

2. What makes you choose the clothes you wear? Do you find yourself pressured to wear certain things to fit in? Do you feel like you wear too much? Or you wear too little? Write your truth.

____

____

____

____

____

3. Do you wear weave? Have you spent money you didn't have to purchase your hair? Do you feel less confident without your weave? Do you love your own hair? Why or Why not? Write your truth.

____
____
____
____
____

4. Do you wear lipstick? If so what drives your color choices? Have you ever put on a lipstick color and felt uncomfortable and said this isn't for me, but wore it anyway? What made you do that? Do you feel pressured by trends to wear colors you wouldn't pick for yourself?

____
____
____
____
____

5. Why are bags (purses) and shoes so important to you? Do you feel like these purchases validate who you are? Are you any less of an individual without these purchases? Write your truth.

____

____

____

____

____

6. How do you defy the expectations society has put on your life? Write your truth.

____

____

____

____

____

7. Who are you? What do you like about yourself? What makes
    you unique? What are some improvements you could make?
    Write your truth.

    ____

    ____

    ____

    ____

    ____

8. What can you do right now to change your present situation
    regarding this topic?

    ____

    ____

    ____

    ____

    ____

My thoughts / revelations about what I wrote in this section…

Additional Thoughts / Reflections

Additional Thoughts / Reflections

Keeping It 100:
You Gotta Stop Living a Lie

1. Have you done things that you are not proud of for material gain? Did you feel some sense of regret? Why or Why not? Write your truth.

____

____

____

____

____

2. Are you currently a Right Now Girl? Have you ever been a Right Now Girl? Do you believe that Right Now Girls exist? What is your personal view of Right Now Girls? Write your truth.

____

____

____

____

____

3. Have you been in a situation with someone who said they cared about you, but acted differently? What is love? In the Early morning hours/ late night hours do you feel like you aren't being totally honest with yourself? Write your truth.

____

____

____

____

____

4. Are you making yourself believe that someone cares about you? Write your truth.

____

____

____

____

5. Do you substitute materials things for care and concern?
    Write your truth.

____

____

____

____

____

6. Do you know your worth? What does this mean to you?
    Write your truth.

____

____

____

____

____

7. Do you have another journal? If not. Get one immediately! If you do what do you use it for? Is it a form of therapy? Write your truth.

____

____

____

____

____

8. What can you do right now to change your present situation regarding this topic?

____

____

____

____

____

My thoughts / revelations about what I wrote in this section…

Additional Thoughts / Reflections

Additional Thoughts / Reflections

Keeping It 100:
The baby is not the End

1. Do you have children? Do you secretly want to have children? Do you feel like you need someone to love or someone to love you unconditionally? Write your truth.

    ____

    ____

    ____

    ____

    ____

2. Do you understand the responsibility of having children? What are those responsibilities? Do you think it is difficult to have children? Do you have a village to support you with the rearing of your children? Write your truth.

    ____

    ____

    ____

    ____

    ____

2. If you already have a baby were you ready to have a baby?
    If you don't have any children do you feel like you are ready
    for children? Write your truth.

    ____
    ____
    ____
    ____
    ____

3. What personal changes have you made for your children?
    Write your truth.

    ____
    ____
    ____
    ____
    ____

4. What sacrifices have you made for your child/ren? Write your truth.

____

____

____

____

____

5. Do you think that your child/ren were a mistake? _ARE YOU AWARE THAT GOD DOES NOT MAKE MISTAKES._ Do you feel like your child/ren have made your life more difficult? Write your truth.

____

____

____

____

____

6. Have you sought out resources to better your life and your child/ren's lives? Have you researched ways to improve your way of life? Write your truth.

____

____

____

____

____

7. What can you do right now to change your present situation regarding this topic?

____

____

____

____

____

My thoughts / revelations about what I wrote in this section…

Additional Thoughts / Reflections

Additional Thoughts / Reflections

Keeping It 100:
Say No to the Influence of Drugs

1. Do you feel like drugs are being commonly used in our society? Do you feel like there is a pressure for you to use drugs? Do you drink alcohol? Do you smoke marijuana? Do you use any other forms of drugs? Write your truth.

____

____

____

____

____

2. Do drugs alter your thinking? Do you make sound decisions under the influence of drugs? Do you feel like your "best" self under the influence of drugs? Write your truth.

____

____

____

____

____

3. What affects do drug usage have on your body? Are you ready to shorten the years of your life because of drug usage? Write your truth.

____

____

____

____

____

4. Are you trying to escape reality by using drugs? Is there an issue that "goes away" when you are under the influence of drugs? What is that issue? Why do you feel that way? Is this a reoccurring thought or issue? Write your truth.

____

____

____

____

____

5. Are you a functioning addict? Have you learned to use drugs and still do all of your normal daily routines? Has drug usage become a everyday part of your life? Write your truth.

____

____

____

____

____

6. Do your "friends" try to influence you to use drugs? Do you think you need a new circle of friends? Are your friends helping you to pursue positivity or negativity? Write your truth.

____

____

____

____

____

7. Do you listen to music that encourages drug usage? Do you ever have "sessions" where you smoke and drink to "trap" music? Do you believe that this music could be entering your spirit and causing you to desire the things that you do not want or need for your life? What are you missing out on by choosing the influence of drugs over living the life God has for you? Write your truth.

____

____

____

____

____

8. What can you do right now to change your present situation regarding this topic? Write your truth.

____

____

____

____

____

My thoughts / revelations about what I wrote in this section…

Additional Thoughts / Reflections

Additional Thoughts / Reflections

Keeping It 100:
Sex or No Sex: That is the Question

1. Are you a virgin? Have you had sex? What was the reason you had sex? How did you feel after having sex? Write your truth.

    ____

    ____

    ____

    ____

    ____

2. Did you feel pressured by your circle of "friends" to have sex? Did you have sex, because "everybody" was doing it? Write your truth.

    ____

    ____

    ____

    ____

    ____

3. Did you know your body is a Holy Temple? Did you know that **EVERYONE** you have sex with leaves a piece of themselves with you, and in order for you to be whole you have to break those connections in the spirit? Have you ever wanted to stop talking to someone you had sex with, but didn't quite know how? Write your truth.

____

____

____

____

____

4. DID YOU KNOW THAT GOD FORGIVES ALL SIN, AND YOU CAN RE-DEDICATE YOUR LIFE AND BODY TO HIM AT ANY MOMENT? (We all make mistakes don't let it hinder you from a life with God) Do you want to re-dedicate your body to God? Write your truth.

____

____

____

____

____

5. Are you tired of feeling "used all up"? Do you feel like people just take, take, take, and never give? Write your truth.

____

____

____

____

____

6. Are you ready to make the decision to live a life Holy and acceptable unto God? Do you want to break ties with people in your life that mean you no good? Do you know how to keep yourself out of compromising situations? Write your truth.

____

____

____

____

____

7. Make a list of all of the people who you have had sexual contact with. (on a separate sheet of paper) Ask God to release you from them, and for him to release them from you. Have Faith! Then tear up the list, and burn it! Forgive yourself, and know that you may fall, but you NEVER stay down! Get back up!! Do you know that you are free? Write your truth.

____

____

____

____

____

8. What can you do right now to change your present situation regarding this topic?

____

____

____

____

____

My thoughts / revelations about what I wrote in this section…

Additional Thoughts / Reflections

Additional Thoughts / Reflections

Keeping It 100:
Coming Out of the Closet

1. Have you had dark moments in your life? Have you ever felt like this was it your life has to be over? What happened? What made you feel this way? Write your truth.

    ____

    ____

    ____

    ____

    ____

2. Where do you go in your dark moments? Do you sit in the closet? Do you lay in the bed? Do you cry in your car? What places do retreat to cope with your hardships? Write your truth.

    ____

    ____

    ____

    ____

    ____

3. Are you depressed? Do you have days when you feel like life is not worth living? Do you feel like bad things just keep happening to you? Write your truth.

____

____

____

____

____

4. Do you love yourself completely? Do you know that you are forgiven? Do you know that NOTHING lasts forever? Do you accept forgiveness for yourself? Write your truth.

____

____

____

____

____

5. How do you get out of the darkness? You say out of your mouth that you are done! You say it EVERYDAY ALLDAY until it comes to pass. Ask God to take away your pain. Write your truth.

____

____

____

____

____

6. What place did you retreat to in your dark moments? Go to that place and declare that it is a place of happiness and peace. Refuse to be sad. You are now a pillar of light! Receive it and Believe it! Write your truth.

____

____

____

____

____

7. Will your hurt end IMMEDIATELY? I would do you a
    complete disservice to say YES!! This will take work on your
    part. Every time you feel that sadness rise up you have to
    change your thinking to the light and love of God. Write
    your truth.

    ____

    ____

    ____

    ____

    ____

8. What can you do right now to change your present situation
    regarding this topic?

    ____

    ____

    ____

    ____

    ____

My thoughts / revelations about what I wrote in this section…

Additional Thoughts / Reflections

Additional Thoughts / Reflections

Keeping It 100:
Alone in a Crowded Room

1. How is it possible to be alone in a crowded room? Have you ever been around a lot of people and felt completely out of place? Where was it? How did you feel? Write your truth.

    ____

    ____

    ____

    ____

    ____

2. Do you have many "friends"? Are your "friends" interested in things that you are no longer interested in? Do you feel ostracized? Write your truth.

    ____

    ____

    ____

    ____

    ____

3. Do you feel like you have been growing apart from people? Do you feel bad for not wanting to do the things you used to do? Do you feel like the "odd man out"? Write your truth.

____

____

____

____

____

4. Do you know what a wilderness experience is? Look up the definition of wilderness. Are you in "new" territory? Write your truth.

____

____

____

____

____

5. Are you ready to say you don't fit in anymore? Are you ready to say that you stand out? Are you ready to be God's light on Earth? Write your truth.

____

____

____

____

____

6. Do you know you are being prepared for a new thing? Look up the definition of prepare. Write your truth.

____

____

____

____

____

7. Do you feel uncomfortable? What is making you uncomfortable? Do you think that the uncomfortableness can be for your good? Change is uncomfortable, but necessary for growth. Write your truth.

____

____

____

____

____

8. What can you do right now to change your present situation regarding this topic?

____

____

____

____

____

My thoughts / revelations about what I wrote in this section…

Additional Thoughts / Reflections

Additional Thoughts / Reflections

Keeping It 100:
Find the God in Me

1. Now what? What are your supposed to do? What do you think you are supposed to do? What do you think is next? Have you asked God? Write your truth.

   ____

   ____

   ____

   ____

   ____

2. Have you joined a local church? Do you stream church online? Do you go to bible study? Do you stream bible study? Are you chasing after God's word? Write your truth.

   ____

   ____

   ____

   ____

   ____

3. Who do you talk to FIRST when a problem arises? Is it your mother? Is it your father? Is it your best friend? A cousin? Who should you talk to first? Who knows ALL the answers to ALL the questions under the sun? Write your truth.

____

____

____

____

____

4. Are you ready for a relationship with God? Do you know that it requires work? Do you know that the rewards for your work will far surpass anything you've ever experienced in this world? Write your truth.

____

____

____

____

5. Do you know that you are the child of a King? Do you know you that you are royalty? Do you know what royalty is? Look up the definition of King. Look up the definition of royalty. DO you understand your rightful place?

____
____
____
____
____

6. Do you know how to pray? If you don't know how to pray start by just sitting quietly until your body is rested and calm. Then have a conversation with God like you would have with any other person, because God is a living God! Do you know how to express your feelings? Express how you feel to God. How do you feel about talking to God? Write your truth.

____
____
____
____
____

7. Are their things you want differently in your life? Are there aspirations you have for yourself or your life? Are there things you want to stop thinking about or things you wish would happen for you? Talk to God tell him **EVERYTHING** that is on your mind! Write your truth.

____

____

____

____

____

8. What can you do right now to change your present situation regarding this topic?

____

____

____

____

____

My thoughts / revelations about what I wrote in this section…

Additional Thoughts / Reflections

Additional Thoughts / Reflections

Keeping It 100:
Walking in Purpose

1. Do you believe that you were created to do something on this Earth? Something that only YOU can do? Something that God made specifically for you? Write your truth.

   ____

   ____

   ____

   ____

   ____

2. Do you know no matter how old you are 12, 27, 38, 42, 55, or even 80 that God will still do this work in you? Do you know that it is never too late for purpose?

   ____

   ____

   ____

   ____

   ____

3. Do you know what your purpose is? Look up the definition
    of purpose. What does it say? Write your truth.

    ____
    ____
    ____
    ____
    ____

4. What do you think your purpose is? Have you asked God?
    Do you know what questions to ask? What do you think is a
    good question to ask regarding purpose? Write your truth.

    ____
    ____
    ____
    ____
    ____

5. What is the one thing that you do in life that makes you extremely happy? What is the thing that you do SO well? What is the one thing you keep trying to get away from, but it keeps coming back to you? Write your truth.

____

____

____

____

____

6. Do you know that the completion of your assignment means glory for God? Did you know that he gave you the answer to a problem that he needed to be solved in the Earth? Write your truth.

____

____

____

____

____

7. Do you know "If God be for us, who can be against us?" (Romans 8:31 Do you know that you cannot fail at purpose? No matter what the situation looks like IT WILL NOT FAIL!!! Are you ready to do what you were called to do AT ALL COSTS? Write your truth.

____

____

____

____

____

8. What can you do right now to change your present situation regarding this topic?

____

____

____

____

____

My thoughts / revelations about what I wrote in this section…

Additional Thoughts / Reflections

Additional Thoughts / Reflections

Pray this prayer:

God you have transformed me from darkness into a beacon of light. You have allowed me to go through the necessary stages to be able to stand before you today. I trust your Will and your way for my life. Not only am I ready, but I am committed to fully seeing the completion of every assignment that you have given me for this life. I am blessed and honored to be chosen by you to help establish your Kingdom. I am fully aware that the road will be narrow and uneasy, but I am up for the challenge. God if ever I want to turn back please keep me focused on you. Please allow me to continuously walk in love, peace, and purpose. Let me be aware at all times that you cannot be stopped therefore when I am walking in my God defined purpose I cannot be stopped. I cannot give up! And I will not quit! You are with me and in me at all times, and when I am no longer carrying myself you have me in your arms. I declare all of this by the Faith you instilled in me in Jesus mighty name Amen!